Attention, Despicable Me fans!
Look for these items when you read this book.
Can you spot them all?

Dave the minion

Cookie Robot

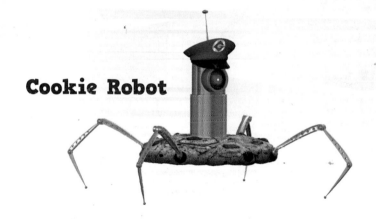

Shrink Ray

Little, Brown and Company · Hachette Book Group · 237 Park Avenue,
New York, NY 10017 · Visit our website at www.lb-kids.com · LB kids is
an imprint of Little, Brown and Company. The LB kids name and logo are
trademarks of Hachette Book Group, Inc.

The publisher is not responsible for websites (or their content)
that are not owned by the publisher.

ISBN: 978-0-316-08382-9 5209 7697 8/13

First edition: May 2010 · 10 9 8 7 6 5

Printed in the U.S.A.

www.despicable.me

My Dad the
Super Villain

Adapted by Lucy Rosen
Based on the Story by Sergio Pablos
Based on the Screenplay by Cinco Paul and Ken Daurio
Illustrated by Rudy Obrero, Charlie Grosvenor,
Peter Moehrle, Dave Williams, and Keith Wong

Gru wanted to be
the world's number-one bad guy.
He lived in a big black house
where he hatched big, despicable plans.

4

Gru's latest plan
was his biggest idea yet.
"Assemble the minions!" he called
as he entered his underground lab.

"Minions, we had a pretty good year
causing crime around the globe,"
Gru told his little workers.
"But next, we are going to do
something even bigger. . . .
We are going to steal the moon!"

There was only one problem.
Gru needed a Shrink Ray to make
the moon small enough to steal.
The only Shrink Ray around
belonged to Gru's nemesis, Vector.

Vector had alarms and booby traps
all over his house.
No one could break in.

Then Gru saw three little girls
outside Vector's house.
They were selling cookies
for the orphanage where they lived.
That gave Gru an idea.

Gru would adopt the girls!
The girls could deliver
boxes filled with Cookie Robots
to help Gru get inside Vector's house
and steal the Shrink Ray.

The girls were named
Margo, Edith, and Agnes.
"Here are the rules," Gru said
when he brought them home.
"You may not touch anything."

"Can we touch the floor?" said Margo.
"What about the air?" she asked.
This was going to be harder
than Gru had thought.

"Girls, let's go!" said Gru.
"Time to deliver the cookies!"
"Okay, but we're going
to dance class first," said Margo.
"We have a big show coming up."

Gru was annoyed.
He did not want to go to dance class.

But Gru went anyway.
"Here you go," said Agnes.
"It's a ticket to the dance show.
You're coming, right?"

"Of course, of course,"
said Gru, rolling his eyes.
"Pinkie promise?" said Agnes.
Gru sighed. "Oh, yes, my pinkie promises."

After dance class, it was time to get
the Shrink Ray from Vector's house.
The girls delivered the cookies.
They did not know that Gru
had hidden his Cookie Robots
inside the cookie boxes.

The Cookie Robots helped Gru
by stealing the Shrink Ray
and handing it off to the minions.
Gru's plan worked perfectly!

Now that Gru had the Shrink Ray,
he was ready to be a full-time villain again.
But he couldn't help
spending time with the girls.

Margo, Edith, and Agnes
wanted to go to Super Silly Fun Land,
so Gru went along for the ride.

The girls tried to win
a stuffed unicorn toy for Agnes,
and Gru lent a hand.

At bedtime,
Gru read the girls a book.
It was called *Sleepy Kittens*.

Before he knew it,
Gru was even having
tea parties with the girls!
The four of them
were becoming a family.

Still, Gru had not forgotten
about his big plan.
At last, he was ready
to steal the moon.

The moon was in
the perfect position for stealing
on the same night
the girls had their dance show.

Gru could either
make his dream come true,
or he could be there
for his new family.

Gru made his choice.
He boarded his rocket ship.
He carefully aimed the Shrink Ray.
The moon got smaller and smaller.

But as Gru grabbed the moon
out of the sky,
he suddenly felt very alone.
His big moment had arrived,
but he had no one to share it with.

Gru remembered all the fun
he had shared with the girls.
And he remembered his
pinkie promise with Agnes.
He knew he had made a mistake.

"I can still make it!" Gru cried
as he turned his ship around.
He got there just in time.

Gru smiled as he took his
new family back home.
Who needs to be
the world's number-one bad guy
when you can be
the world's number-one dad?